SAD

BORED

LUCKY

AFRAID

WITHDRAWN

D0119070

CONFUSED

MAD

?

JEALOUS

How are you feeling today?

HAPPY

EXCITED

GRATEFUL

PROUD

CHEERFUL

THEO'S MOOD

Maryann Cocca-Leffler

ALBERT WHITMAN & COMPANY
CHICAGO, ILLINOIS

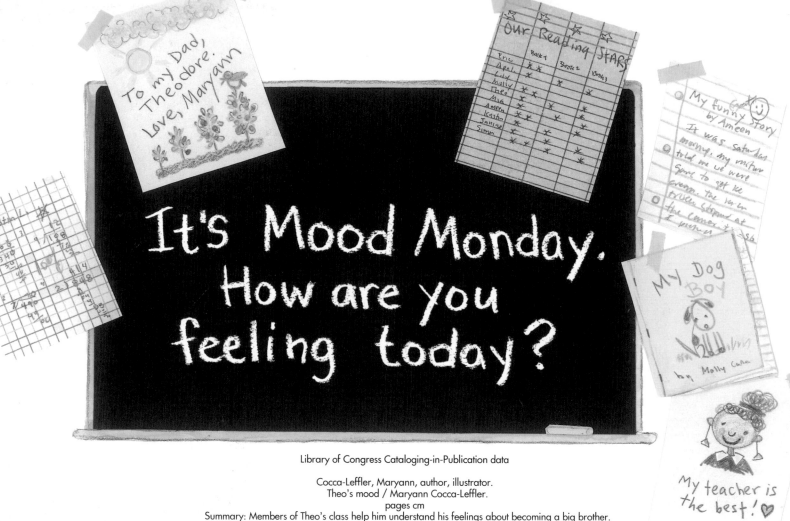

It's Mood Monday.
How are you
feeling today?

Library of Congress Cataloging-in-Publication data

Cocca-Leffler, Maryann, author, illustrator.
Theo's mood / Maryann Cocca-Leffler.
pages cm
Summary: Members of Theo's class help him understand his feelings about becoming a big brother.
ISBN 978-0-8075-7778-3 (alk. paper)
[1. Emotions—Fiction. 2. Brothers and sisters—Fiction. 3. Babies—Fiction. 4. Schools—Fiction.] I. Title.
PZ7.C638The 2013
[E]—dc23
2012049834

Printed in China.
10 9 8 7 6 5 4 3 2 1 BP 18 17 16 15 14 13

For more information about Albert Whitman & Company, visit our web site at www.albertwhitman.com.

The design is by Maryann Cocca-Leffler and Nick Tiemersma.

Please visit Maryann at her web site, www.maryanncoccaleffler.com.

It was Mood Monday and Theo was the first to share his mood news.

"Are you in a good mood or a bad mood?" asked Miss Cady.

"I don't know," said Theo.

BAD MOODS

SAD

BORED

JEALOUS

AFRAID

CONFUSED

MAD

"Well, did anything happen this weekend?" asked Miss Cady.

"My mother had a baby girl," answered Theo.

Everyone cheered. "Theo has a new sister!"

GOOD MOODS

EXCITED

LUCKY

GRATEFUL

PROUD

HAPPY

"That's GOOD MOOD NEWS—isn't it?" asked Miss Cady. "How does it feel to have a new sister, Theo?"

"I don't know," said Theo.

"Maybe you feel **HAPPY** like me," said Eric.

"I got a new bike!"

"Maybe you feel **JEALOUS** like me," said Lily.

"My sister won another trophy."

"Maybe you feel **AFRAID** like me," said Ameen.

"I got lost in the mall."

"Maybe you feel **SAD** like me," said April.

"My dog ran away."

"Maybe you feel **MAD** like me," said Molly.

"My brother ripped my favorite book."

"Maybe you feel **PROUD** like me," said Mia.

"I hit a home run!"

"Well, Theo," the class asked. "How do **you** feel?"
Theo sat…and thought and thought…

Finally he said, "I feel HAPPY.

"My grandma is staying for a whole w

"But I also feel JEALOUS.
Mommy has no time to play with me.

"And I feel
AFRAID.
I don't want

"And I feel **SAD.** I'm not my daddy's 'one and only.'

"And I feel **MAD.** I can't play my drum when the baby is sleeping.

SSSHHHHH

"But how can you feel all those feelings
at the same time?" asked the kids.

SAD

AFRAID

MAD

"Because," said Theo,
"I FEEL LIKE A BIG BROTHER!"

JEALOUS

HAPPY

PROUD

SAD

BORED

LUCKY

AFRAID

MAD

CONFUSED

?

JEALOUS

How are you feeling today?

HAPPY

EXCITED

GRATEFUL

PROUD

CHEERFUL